Andra, the Selfish Unicorn

Lynda Osborne

For Victoria

Thanks to Trisha for her help with

revision

Chapter One

Flaunia's dress of pressed flowers and leaves skimmed the top of the long grass as she walked. Creatures of the Forest and Glade stopped what they were doing to watch as she passed. Many of them bowed their heads as she smiled at them, for Flaunia was the Green Fairy. The Green Fairy of the Forest and Glade, she was their guardian and their protector.

Pausing for a moment, Flaunia looked around. The glade was calm and peaceful, but to her skilled eye, she could see the first signs of autumn. The tips of leaves rustling in the gentle breeze were starting to turn brown. Butterflies and bees danced from one flower to the next in the search for pollen and nectar, while the creatures of the Forest and Glade feasted on berries and fruit, fattening themselves to carry them over the colder months. Not that autumn or even winter, for that matter, lasted long here, the Green Fairy saw to that.

Shading her eyes, Flaunia stared into the distance. Her smile broadened as she saw the herd of unicorn waiting to greet her. Spotting Andra, the son of the unicorn king, a frown creased her face as she watched him walking towards the stream, he was as selfish as ever, pushing pushed past the younger golden foals and their mothers to get to the cool water first.

"Andra!" She called.

Hearing his name, the young unicorn threw up his head and whinnied. Catching sight of Flaunia he trotted towards her, his long spiral horn sparkled and the diamonds in his front hooves twinkled as they caught the sun.

Even from this distance, the Green Fairy could see the gold and silver flecks in his coat, distinguishing him from the foals and the pure white adults as a juvenile.

"Andra!"

The young unicorn snorted, tossing his head as he approached. Flaunia looked cross. From the tone in her voice, he wondered what he had done wrong this time.

Flaunia started to speak as the young unicorn approached.

"Andra, as the future leader of the herd, I gave you a name to reflect your position and future status. Your name means strong and courageous..."

Andra interrupted the Green Fairy with a stamp of his hoof; after all, he had heard this before... more than once!

Flaunia continued, ignoring the unicorn's tantrum, annoying him even more.

"You know the leader of the herd must be strong and courageous, especially as the human world creeps ever closer to our own."

The unicorn nodded, it was true, his father was the bravest unicorn he had ever met.

The Green Fairy smiled, it was obvious Andra loved and respected his father deeply.

"But as well as strong and courageous, you must be kind... considerate and helpful, especially protective of the younger or weaker members of the herd. Lead by example, prove you are someone the rest of the herd can respect and look up to."

She paused for a moment, gathering her thoughts, she took the opportunity to look round and enjoy the peace and tranquillity of the glade.

"We both know you can be mean and spiteful. Look how you push the young foals out of your way to get to the best grass, or drink from the stream first… and before you argue, I've seen you do it time after time."

Andra dipped his head, trying to hide his embarrassment, too ashamed to admit what the Green Fairy said was true.

He was the son of the leader of the herd. He thought to himself, trying to justify his actions. *Why shouldn't the lower ranked unicorns give way to him?*

His embarrassment faded away as he defended his actions to himself, leaving him as proud and selfish as usual.

Flaunia shook her head, a look of sadness darkening her face. Andra would be leader of the herd all too soon. He had to learn a lesson in kindness and compassion and she had to teach him that lesson quickly.

Thoughtfully, the Green Fairy stroked her chin, smiling as an idea came to her, but her smile was one of sorrow. She wasn't looking forward to what she had to do.

Raising her arms above her head. The long sleeves of her gown slipped down to her elbows as she waved her hands over the young unicorn and clicked her fingers.

For a moment, nothing happened. The sound of bees buzzing and birds singing in the nearby trees filled the air. In the distance, unicorn foals whinnied to one another as they played. Andra shook his head, his silken mane flying as he snorted, trying not to laugh. Flaunia raised her eyebrows as she started to speak.

"Unicorn young, unicorn selfish, a lifelong lesson for you I wish. Courage you have. Strength too. But humility and kindness are traits far too few. I banish you now, to a place far from here. But will welcome you back when you discover the true you."

Surrounded by smoke, Andra started to spin as he fell head over heels through the air, landing in a heap on the ground. Embarrassed, the unicorn scrambled to his feet in an undignified manner, glancing around to make sure no-one had seen what had happened.

Everything was different.

Where was Flaunia?

Where was the herd?

Andra felt sick with fear... he had no idea where he was.

Overhead, the clear blue sky was gone, replaced by one that was grey, studded with black storm clouds chasing one another across the heavens, bounced along by gusts of wind. The sounds of the glade were gone. All he could hear was the noise of waves crashing onto nearby rocks, showering him with salty spray. He shivered as the wind howled around him, where was he? The young unicorn spun round, as a sense of panic gripped him.

Where was the Green Fairy?

Where was the Glade?

Where was the herd?

The questions spun round and round in his head as he looked around. The yellow sand underfoot stretched in every direction until it reached some rugged cliffs towering overhead. Above, a seagull soared, its beady eyes scouring the beach for something to eat.

In the distance, Andra noticed a group of scruffy, stubby legged ponies. They were not unicorns, but they could tell him where he was. Whinnying a greeting, he trotted towards them.

Chapter Two

With his tail kinked high over his back, and his ears flicked forward, Andra trotted across the sand. The ponies look up as he approached, *they must be admiring his beautiful horn or the diamonds in his hooves,* he thought to himself. But they were more interested in eating a type of green-slimy looking plant washed up by the waves than admiring him.

Reaching the scruffy ponies, he waited for them to say hello, but instead, they ignored him as they concentrated on grazing. Andra was confused. It was as if a unicorn amongst them was normal. Instead of grazing, they should be showing him the respect he thought he deserved, after all he was the future leader of the unicorns.

Andra cleared his throat. "Um, excuse me?"

The closest pony, a small grey filly, looked up, a long piece of seaweed hanging from her mouth.

"C...can you tell me where I can find my herd...?" He asked, "urm, please?" He added as an afterthought.

"What herd?" She asked, her voice muffled as her mouth was crammed with seaweed.

"Unicorns. A herd of unicorns just like me."

The other ponies stopped grazing and stared at the stranger.

Unicorns? They must have mis-heard.

Nah, that couldn't be right, there was no such thing as a unicorn!

The grey filly started to laugh.

"Ha ha, unicorns don't exist. Everyone knows that," she giggled.

"Yes, they do!" Andra exclaimed. "Look at me!" He said, stamping his hoof in indignation. "I am a unicorn."

Confused, the grey filly shook her head.

"Yeah right, I'm not sure when you last looked at your reflection but it's obvious to me, you're a Shetland pony, just like the rest of us."

Her voice was quiet, but kind, unlike the other ponies whose rude, loud laughter was ringing in his ears.

Andra looked down at himself. His long slender, silver legs had disappeared, replaced by short stubby ones covered in thick matted hair, just like the herd of ponies. Moreover, where were the diamonds which studded his front hooves? Something was wrong. This wasn't right.

Andra went boss-eyed as he tried to catch a glimpse of his beautiful spiral horn, but that too was gone. In fact, all he could see was his once silky mane, which was now as matted as the ponies he had been speaking to, blown over his eyes by the latest gust of wind. It was no good, he had to see his reflection. He had to be sure he wasn't as ugly as these ponies.

He trotted away, the sound of the ponies' laughter ringing in his ears. Angry, Andra pressed into a canter and hurried along the beach. Spotting a rock pool, he headed over. The surface of the water rippled with tiny waves, whipped up by the breeze. He waited. At last the wind dropped long enough for the water to settle allowing him to see his reflection.

He lent over the pool and stared into the depths of the rock pool.

The young unicorn pulled back, his eyes were playing tricks on him. That was not his reflection. He snatched another peek. No, he hadn't imagined it, a scruffy pony stared back at him from the depths of the rock pool. Something was very wrong. His beautiful flecked coat was gone. So was his stunning conical horn. Instead, a Shetland pony stared back. A thick mane of brown and white hair flopped over his face as he twisted to get a better look at himself, neighing in alarm at what he saw. His coat was covered in brown and white patches. He wasn't even one colour... It wasn't fair! A large, warm tear ran down his face, dripping off the end of his nose and shattering the surface of the water, wiping out his horrible reflection in a series of ripples.

This had to be the work of the Green Fairy. She had told him he was mean and selfish. It was her way of teaching him the lesson she said he had to learn, but that didn't matter now, all he could think about was getting back to the Glade and his herd. But there was one problem – he had no idea where he was or how he was going to get home.

Andra snuck another look at his reflection now that the surface had settled. He shuddered. How could Flaunia have done this to him? Yes, without a doubt, she had turned him into a small, clumsy and very, very ugly Shetland pony.

Chapter Three

He could not bear to look at himself. With his head hung so low his nose almost touched the sand, he walked back towards the herd of ponies. They may be as ugly as he was, but he didn't want to be alone.

The small grey filly stopped eating as he approached.

"Hello again," she said. "You didn't go far," she observed.

Andra didn't answer. He knew he was being rude, but he had nothing to say. He was frightened, lost and had nowhere else to go. But at least he wasn't alone.

The grey filly shrugged.

"Don't talk if you don't want to," she said, watching him for a moment before snatching another mouthful of the green slimy plant she was eating.

A black stallion walked over. He was a little taller than the other ponies, but he had the same thick coat and his mane and tail was as matted as theirs, but there was something different about him, he reminded Andra of his father. The other ponies moved aside as he passed, just as the members of the herd did when his father walked by. It was clear he was their leader.

Andra watched the stallion approach. His eyes were cold, and his nostrils flared as he snorted. Andra nervously looked away, did the black pony think he was going to make a challenge for the herd? That was the last thing on the unicorn's mind. He was cold, tired and very hungry. All he wanted was to get home, fast. With luck, he wasn't going to be here long enough to form friendships, let alone challenge the leader of the herd.

"That's Jet," whispered the grey filly as she stepped aside.

Andra nodded his thanks as the stallion walked closer, never taking his eyes off the young unicorn. As the leader, it was his job to protect his herd and see off any challenger.

Andra stepped backwards. He bowed as low as he could, his eyes screwed tight shut, wishing he were somewhere else. He didn't want to cause trouble of any sort - he was in enough of that without adding to his problems.

Jet took another step towards the unicorn. Andra continued to back away, his actions slow and deliberate. He had to make sure Jet knew he wasn't a threat.

For a long moment, Jet stared at the new arrival, never taking his eyes off him. Andra kept his head bowed. He took another step backwards. He wanted to keep a big gap between Jet and himself.

At last the stallion was satisfied this newcomer wasn't a challenger, Jet stamped his hoof before rearing onto his hind legs, not that he needed to do that, the stranger had backed

away, but he wanted to make a point. He

wasn't to be meddled with, and he was going to

make sure the stranger knew his place.

At any other time, Andra would have

found the situation funny. His father would

never see off a challenger in this way. But

then, come to think of it, no one had ever

challenged his father, he was such a good, kind

leader.

Andra threw the black pony a quick

glance, sighing with relief as he saw the stallion

had started to graze. The sight of the herd

eating reminded the young unicorn how hungry

he was. His stomach rumbled loudly. He

watched the ponies as they browsed. It didn't

look very tasty but there didn't seem to be anything else. He took a mouthful of the slimy plant and gave it a quick chew.

"Yuk!" He spat out the half-chewed food, a look of disgust flashing across his face. The plant was wet and as slimy as it looked, and to top it all, it was so salty it made him feel sick – it was the worst thing he had ever tasted.

Andra rolled his eyes as the grey filly wandered over. She seemed determined to be his friend.

"I'm Blue," she said.

The unicorn nodded. "Hi, I'm Andra," he replied.

Blue smiled. "That's a strange name. Andra," she repeated, "Andra. Mmm, I like it though."

Andra couldn't help smiling, "Thanks... I think."

"You're not from round here, aren't you?" She asked, continuing to speak without waiting for him to respond. "You look like one of us, a Shetland pony, I mean, but there is something very strange about you."

Andra shrugged, "I'm not too sure where I come from, not that you'd believe me even if I told you." He pawed at the seaweed. "Is this all there is to eat?"

"It's not great is it? But you'll get used to it after a while, though I've never met a Shetland pony who hasn't been brought up on seaweed."

That's because I'm not a Shetland pony! Andra thought, ignoring the rumbling in his tummy.

He realised if he was to find a way home, he wouldn't find it here on the beach. He had to explore.

The unicorn glanced over his shoulder. Jet and the other ponies were grazing, while Blue insisted on hovering around him. She seemed a nice girl, but he had to get rid of her, even though she was the only one to have shown him any kindness since he arrived. He didn't want to be nasty if he could help it, but he didn't want her hanging around.

"Blue, I have to go."

"Where?" She asked her voice eager.

Andra tossed his head, "Oh here and there."

"Oh, I've never been here and there," she replied, "can I come?"

Andra looked up at the sky, this was going to be more difficult than he thought.

"Please?"

Andra shrugged and started to walk away. Blue remained where she was for a moment before trotting after him.

This went on for a few minutes, leaving Andra feeling meaner as each minute ticked by. Slowly it dawned on him, she just wanted to help, perhaps she could show him around. Maybe it wasn't such a bad idea to have her around after all.

Andra spun round with more force than he intended, causing Blue to pull up sharply, her small hooves sliding on the wet sand.

"Why did you do that?" She demanded. It was clear from the tone his quick actions had frightened her.

"Sorry," said Andra, blushing. "It's just... well, if you are going to follow me like a shadow, we might as well go together."

"Oh," Blue couldn't keep the surprise out of her voice, she was expecting him to chase her off. "Good, let's get going," she said, taking the lead.

Andra choked back a laugh but followed the small filly. For the first time since arriving in this awful place he felt a genuine smile form on his lips. Perhaps Shetland ponies weren't all bad.

Chapter Four

Andra scuffed his hooves in the sandy soil as he dragged one in front of another. He was exhausted. It seemed as if they had been walking for ages.

Spotting a small patch of grass, Blue and Andra bumped noses as they both leant forward to graze. Blushing, Blue pulled back, as Andra snatched a mouthful before leaving the rest for her. He chewed a couple of times, it was better than seaweed but didn't taste anything like the sweet fresh grass of the Glade. Despite walking inland, he could still taste the salt which seemed to coat everything here, but it was better than nothing, at least it would stop his tummy rumbling for a little while.

Perhaps, Flaunia would think he had learnt his lesson – whatever the lesson was she wanted him to learn. He was desperate to go home. He missed his parents, he missed the Glade, he smiled as he admitted to himself, he even missed the foals, even though they annoyed him and were always getting in his way.

However, the Green Fairy was nowhere to be seen.

Andra shivered, if Flaunia wasn't coming back for him today, he'd have to find shelter. He didn't like the look of the sky; it was darker than when he had first arrived. It was hard to understand how anywhere could be so cold and unwelcoming, even during the coldest part of the Glade's short winter, it never rained for longer than a few minutes at a time, and the sun was always close by.

He shuddered, more from fear than cold, but at that moment he was even grateful for his thick coat despite the fact it looked such a mess.

"Blue."

The grey filly turned to face him. For the first time, Andra looked at her for more than a second. There was something about her. She wasn't pretty, just different. Andra couldn't help staring at the young filly while he tried to figure out what he liked about her... ah, that was it, she had 'funny' eyes. Each was a different colour. One was as dark as his, the other, light blue. He smiled as it dawned on him why she was called Blue.

"Thanks for looking out for me," he said.

Blue shrugged.

"T'was fine. I had nothing better to do," she said, her voice low, almost shy.

"Where, um, where are we?"

Blue was puzzled.

"What do you mean?"

Andra wrinkled his nose. To him the question was obvious, but he bit his tongue, he needed her help, he didn't want to get in trouble for being rude.

"Here," he said, tossing his head in a vague direction. "What's this place called?"

Blue pulled a face.

"Shetland. This is one of the Shetland Islands, um, we are Shetland ponies."

Andra nodded, "Ah yes, of course you are, but I'm a unicorn."

"Oh yeah, I keep forgetting," Blue replied, she kept her voice light though it was difficult not to sound sarcastic.

"You... you do believe me?"

"Yeah, of course I do. It's... well... I've never seen a unicorn, and to be honest, I don't know anyone who has."

"Well, you do now," he said.

"Blue... Bluey..."

The ponies turned at the sound of the filly's name.

Andra felt sick. A small human was running towards them, at least that's what he thought was running up to them.

The Green Fairy had told him time and time again that humans were dangerous, they couldn't be trusted. Over thousands of years they had taken nearly all the land belonging to the fairies and magical creatures. Flaunia insisted human creatures must never enter the Glade, and never learn of the existence of unicorns.

"Who's that?" He asked his voice thick with fear.

Blue swished her tail and started to walk towards the small human.

"Blue," he called, his voice urgent, trying to ignore the stories of humans hunting unicorns to the point of extinction. If the Green Fairy hadn't rescued the last few unicorn's, they would have disappeared long ago.

"What's wrong," Blue hissed. "Don't tell me you've never seen a little girl before?" She asked, surprised at the look of fear that flashed across her new friend's face. "Andra, don't be daft," she urged, "it's just Carrie." She sounded excited, as if this small human was a friend, someone she trusted.

After a moment, Andra started to follow, but kept his distance as the young filly walked with confidence towards Carrie.

As the child came closer, Andra stared at her with interest. She had short ginger hair, which seemed to have a mind of its own, jutting out at angles as if it couldn't make friends with a brush or a comb.

Her mop of hair framed a round face, with a ruddy complexion, no doubt from the constant wind and rain – there was even a smear of dirt across her cheek. She was dressed in a pair of faded, patched dungarees, the right strap held in place by a large safety pin. In a funny sort of way this small human reminded him of Flaunia. Not from the way she looked, she certainly wasn't pretty, and her clothes were nothing like the silken gown spun from flowers and leaves worn by the Green Fairy, but there was an air of kindness about her, just like Flaunia.

Reaching the girl, Cassie flung her arms around the pony's neck and showered her with kisses.

"Blue, I haven't seen you for days!" Cassie exclaimed, burying her face deeper into the pony's shaggy coat.

Blue whinnied to Andra, trying to coax him to join them, but he seemed unwilling to come closer.

Cassie patted Blue's hindquarters before pulling some burrs from her tail.

"And who's this?" She asked, looking straight at Andra. "Hello," she said, her tone gentle.

The little human held her hand out towards Andra, her fingers tucked in, just as her father had taught her when she was very small. That way the ponies couldn't nip them by accident. She stretched her arm out, so Andra might catch her scent, let him know she wasn't going to hurt him.

Andra strained his neck, too nervous to take a step closer, but couldn't resist the urge to give her a sniff.

He knew Flaunia would be angry when she learnt how close he'd come to the girl, but he'd love telling the foals he'd sniffed the outstretched hand of a little human…Wow! What a tale to tell, though he'd leave out the bit about being nervous.

Andra edged forward and sniffed the small-outstretched hand, his movements slow, deliberate. He sniffed again, her skin smelt sweet, but he pulled back as she went to touch him.

"Whoa, easy laddie," Cassie murmured.

Andra's ears twitched as she spoke.

"Come on laddie," Cassie urged. "Don't be frightened. I'm not going to hurt you."

Blue nudged her friend.

"For goodness sake, Cassie won't hurt you," she hissed under her breath.

"There's a good lad," the girl repeated.

Andra trembled as he allowed Cassie to touch him.

"There, that didn't hurt, did it?" She said, continuing to speak all the time her hand had contact with his brown and white neck. "Good lad," she mumbled. "I don't think I've seen you before," she continued, "and I thought I knew all the ponies on the island." A frown clouded her face for a moment before being replaced by a soft smile. "No matter, I'd better give you a name. Let me see, ah yes, I'm going to call you Patch."

Patch? Andra thought. *My name is Andra*, he wanted to shout but he knew she wouldn't be able to understand him.

"Cassie gives us all names," Blue explained.

"But 'Patch'. Really? That's awful," he grumbled.

Blue smiled, "I don't know what you are moaning about, she called my cousin, Brown Tail," she giggled.

Andra couldn't help smiling.

"Mmm, you're right, that is worse."

With slow, deliberate movements, Cassie reached into her pocket, pulling out a long orange vegetable, which she snapped in half.

"Carrot?" She asked. "But don't tell Mum. This was meant to go into the stew pot this evening."

She placed one half on her open palm and offered it to Blue who, with care, picked it off the small, outstretched hand. Cassie giggled as the pony's whiskery chin tickled her fingers. She repeated the process, this time offering the other half to Andra.

Andra resisted the urge to snatch the carrot. He had never tasted one before, but he knew it had to be better than the slimy seaweed he had eaten on the beach. He bit down onto the crisp vegetable and chewed. *Mmm, I like carrots!*

Her movements slow and deliberate, Cassie reached out and stroked his neck, his skin twitching under her touch. This was the first time he had ever been touched by someone other than the Green Fairy.

"Cassie!"

The small human looked up.

"Coming, Mum," she called, her voice snatched by a gust of wind.

"Cassie, come on in, love. It'll be dark soon."

"Coming," Cassie repeated, this time a little louder.

She turned to go, giving Blue a final pat on as she passed, stopping after a few steps.

"Come on," she urged. "Come and sleep in the barn, no one will know," she added, her voice little more than a whisper. "There's no food, but it will be warmer than spending the night in the open. Come on, Blue...Patch, come on." She clicked her tongue, urging the ponies to follow her.

Blue didn't need to be told again. She was happy to follow the small human, but Andra wasn't so sure, he had no idea what a barn was.

"Come on," Blue hissed, neighing in frustration as Andra refused to move. This unicorn, or whatever he wanted to be called, was strange – very strange indeed.

Chapter Five

Not wanting to be left alone, Andra waited a couple of minutes before trotting after his friend. Spotting the run-down barn, he stopped dead in his tracks. He had never seen anything like it. Well, if he was honest, this was the first building he had ever seen. It was a squat, rectangular structure built from stone. A tatty hessian sack, flapping in the wind like a flag, covered the hole where the window had once been, its glass had been broken years ago and never replaced. The roof was made of corrugated iron, its once smooth, furrowed surface had rusted with age. Plants more often found clinging to the island's cliffs had seeded themselves into the building's crumbling mortar, and the wooden door was rotting and need of immediate repair before it fell off its one remaining hinge.

The young unicorn whinnied in alarm, startled by the sound of the roof rattling in the wind. Blue tried to encourage him forward with a gentle nudge as Cassie walked towards them with peelings from the carrots, potato and swede her mother was cooking for their evening meal.

Andra watched while the little human brushed Blue. She was careful not to remove too much mud from the pony's grey coat as it helped to keep her warm. Even he had to admit, the filly looked pretty when the small human had finished.

Cassie divided the vegetable peelings into two and placed half in front of Blue and half in front of the young unicorn. Andra snatched a mouthful, giving them a quick chew before swallowing.

"Right," said Cassie, keeping her tone low. "Let's have a look at you," she said, placing the brush with care against Andra's neck. A frown darkened her face as she felt him tremble under her touch. This puzzled her, all the ponies were familiar with human contact, or so she thought. Many were handled from birth, and she had spent countless hours befriending the herd that wandered across her father's land.

"Whoa, easy there, Patch," she whispered, his ears flicking as she spoke.

The sound of her voice was not as soothing as Flaunia's, but it was soft and kind. He hated to admit it, but perhaps this little human wasn't as bad as he expected.

Absorbed in his own thoughts, Andra didn't hear the barn door creak as it was pushed closed. Someone had joined them in the barn.

Cassie's mother stood with her back to the door drying her hands on the front of her apron. She was a taller version of her daughter, they had the same ginger hair, in the older woman's case, worn as a plait down her back, where as her daughter's hair was an unruly mop, which was never tamed, no matter what her mother did to try to tidy it up. She chuckled as she watched Cassie. Her daughter loved all animals, but the ponies were by far her favourite. It amused her when Cassie 'smuggled' the occasional vegetable from the larder or begged for the peelings to feed her beloved ponies.

"Who have you got hidden in here?" She asked, "I can see Blue, but I don't recognise the skewbald," she said, nodding towards the brown and white pony.

Andra, alarmed by the sound of the unfamiliar voice backed away, his nostrils flaring. He had almost accepted the small human, but this was too much...

"Whoa laddie," Cassie murmured, throwing her arm around Andra's neck, she thought in a reassuring way, but it panicked the unicorn, his body stiffening as he pulled away.

"Ahh, Mum, he's frightened of you."

Her mother nodded, "I can see that, Cassie. I don't think I've ever seen a pony react like this. Where did you find him?"

Cassie shrugged, "Dunno, He was with Blue."

"What's wrong?" Blue hissed through gritted teeth.

Andra shook his head. "It's... it's the humans," he stuttered, "Fl... Flaunia says they're dangerous."

Blue tossed her head and laughed. *Carrie, dangerous*, that was the silliest thing she had heard for a long time.

"Who is Flaunia?" She demanded.

"The Green Fairy," replied Andra, his tone thick with surprise, *surely it was obvious?* But a glance at Blue's expression told him she didn't have a clue who he was talking about. He sighed deeply before continuing. "Flaunia is our guardian. She is the Green Fairy of Forest and Glade," his tone softening as he spoke, perhaps realising for the first time what the fairy meant to him.

Blue stamped her hoof. This nonsense had gone on long enough.

"There is no such thing as fairies!" She retorted. "Or elves, pixies, ghosties or ghouls," she added for good measure. "And while I think about it, there's no such thing as unicorns either. I played along with your little game, but you have gone too far now." She swivelled on the spot and stormed out of the barn, the rickety door swinging on its hinge as she pushed it open.

"Blue!" Carrie called, as the grey filly disappeared, wondering what had spooked her.

Alarmed at being left alone with the 'enemy', as Andra regarded the humans, the unicorn hurried after the filly, pushing past the little girl in such a rush she almost toppled over.

"Cassie..." her mother cried in alarm.

Her daughter laughed, the sound forced. "I'm fine," she lied, hurt that Patch had reacted so badly. "He's a strange lad," she added, "that's for certain."

Andra pushed into a canter as he tried to catch Blue, the wind tugged at his mane and tail as he hurried, causing them to stream out behind him like bunting.

"Blue," he neighed, "Blue, please stop".

The small grey filly pulled up and tugged at the leaves of a small tree, its growth stunted by the near constant wind as he cantered up to her.

Andra, breathing hard, nuzzled her mane. She, along with the small human, were the only ones to show him any kindness since he arrived on the island. Blue was the closest thing he had to a friend.

Sulking, she turned her back on him and pulled another mouthful of leaves from the tree.

"I'm sorry," Andra whispered.

"P-a-r-d-o-n?" She said in an exaggerated fashion, chewing loudly, "I can't hear you."

"I said, I'm sorry,"

"Ok, no need to shout, I'm not deaf." She glanced at him, admittedly, he did look sorry, his expression of shame seemed genuine.

"What can I say?"

"The truth would be nice," she retorted.

"But I... but..." he stammered, torn between making something up just to remain friends with the pony, or telling the truth, knowing she wasn't going to believe him. He inhaled, filling his lungs with the cold salty air. "I was... I am telling the truth. I don't care if you don't believe me, but it is true. I am a unicorn."

Blue rolled her eyes but remained silent.

Andra looked away. He couldn't prove he was telling the truth; he would have to think of a way to make her believe him. *Where was Flaunia when he needed her?* He blinked as tears started to fall.

"Are you crying again?" Blue asked, but the anger had gone from her tone.

Andra shook his head in a brusque manner, "No! It's the wind causing my eyes to water," he lied.

"Yeah, it has a habit of doing that, eh?" She mumbled, nudging him in a playful manner.

Chapter Six

Out of the corner of her eye, Blue noticed Andra shiver.

"Come on," she urged, "let's see if Cassie has left the barn open. You never know we may be lucky."

Andra shook his head, *doubt it*, he thought to himself.

Blue glanced at her friend, she could see the look of uncertainty shadowing his face.

"Cassie's nice," she said.

Andra was silent for a moment before speaking.

"I pushed past her trying to catch up with you. When you left, I panicked at the thought of being so close to the little human and her mother. I-think-I-pushed-her-over." The words gushed from his mouth in a jumble as he hurried to explain his behaviour.

Blue raised her eyebrows, "You are silly, aren't you?"

Andra didn't answer.

"Come on," she urged, "Cassie won't hold it against you. I've said she's nice." She looked at the unicorn for a moment before continuing, "look, stay or come with me, the choice is yours. I know what I'm going to do."

Andra didn't hesitate for long. He could be stubborn, but he wasn't stupid. He wasn't going to let the prospect of shelter from this wind and somewhere a little warmer to sleep pass him by.

Trotting to catch up with his friend, he noticed a movement to the left of him.

"Blue!" He whinnied. "Blue, what's that?" He stopped. There, lying in front of him was one of the strangest creatures he had ever seen. Its black face was bald, or at least covered by very fine hair, but its body was odd. He hadn't seen anything like it before. White curly wool covered the strange creature's body, and it had bald legs sticking out at the corners.

"Blue," he hissed.

Hiding between this strange-looking creature and a wall was another one, a smaller version, shivering as it tried to shield from the wind.

Blue trotted back to the brown and white pony, but there was an air of reluctance about her, she was desperate to get out of the rain.

Andra nodded towards the strange creatures.

"Oh my, that's a lamb and its mother, looks like it's a new-born."

"Lamb, what's a lamb?"

"A baby sheep. The larger creature is a sheep and its baby is a lamb."

"Sheep?" Andra repeated.

Blue nodded.

"I've never seen a sheep, or a lamb before."

Yeah right, she pulled a face, it was getting harder and harder to believe what he was saying. There were hundreds of sheep across the islands, he must have seen them before?

"Look," he said, "the little one is shivering." He took a step closer.

The ewe bleated. It seemed to be asking for help.

Andra glanced at Blue, and back at the sheep. He went to follow his friend, but the ewe bleated again, it was obvious it needed help.

The unicorn shook his head, the rain was causing his mane to stick to his face, making it difficult to see.

"The little one is freezing."

"Oh, come on, they'll be fine," Blue grumbled, eager to return to the barn.

"No, I'm going to see if I can help, can't they come with us to the shelter?"

Blue kissed the back of her teeth. Annoyed, she followed Andra back to the sheep.

Andra tried to nudge the ewe out of the way, but she wasn't having any of it. He may be bigger than she was, but she wasn't moving from her lamb.

"I don't think this little chap will make it to the barn," Andra observed. "You go on, I'm going to stay with them," he urged. "There's no point in us both freezing, it's so wet and cold."

Blue hesitated for a moment, not sure what to do. She was desperate to get out of the cold, but one glance at the tiny lamb and she knew she couldn't leave. With a shake of her head, she followed Andra towards the new family.

Having filled its belly with its mother's milk, the young lamb snuggled against the wall. Its mother settled beside her lamb, but they were getting wetter and colder by the minute.

Together, the ponies lay beside the sheep, trying to get as close to the woolly animals as they could to shield them from the wind and rain spraying them with sand and debris whipped up from the beach. Snuggled between the ponies, it didn't take long for the lamb to stop shivering, warmed by the heat from the bodies of the bigger animals.

Unlike the lamb, Andra couldn't settle. His mind drifted to thoughts of his family, his father, the king of the unicorns and his beautiful mother. He longed to feel his mama's warm breath on his neck as she greeted him each morning. Screwing his eyes tight shut, he wanted to keep that image in his mind for as long as possible, eventually, exhausted, he fell

asleep.

Chapter Seven

Andra sighed, shifting position in his sleep as the lamb snuggled closer to him. Blue smiled to herself. Despite this strange pony's bluster, he seemed to have a good heart. Sheep were so common on the island, she knew she wouldn't have noticed the ewe and her lamb struggling in the cold. To her they were just a part of the scenery, another animal needing a share of the sparse food supply.

At last, the sun peeped over the horizon, bringing with it the promise of better weather. The bright orange orb seemed to float on the calm sea like a child's ball bobbing up and down on a lake. The loud raucous call of a seagull woke Andra with a jolt. His sudden movement dragged Blue from her daydream.

"Morning," she smiled.

Andra blinked once or twice as he tried to focus his bleary eyes,

"Oh hello," he stuttered as his body gave an involuntary shudder. He stumbled to his feet and stretched, allowing the ewe to shift her position and suckle her lamb.

Andra snuffled the lamb with his muzzle, just as his mother had done when he was a youngster. He inhaled the strange scent of the little creature, giggling to himself as its soft curly fleece tickled his nose.

Blue shook her head as she watched her new friend. Everything seemed so new and strange to him, it, well if she was honest, it was as if this was the first time he had been on the island. She glanced away for a moment, frightened to admit there was something magical about him. Oh, she wasn't sure about fairies and unicorns, but he was enchanting.

She whickered to get his attention, the sound soft, friendly. Andra looked up.

"I think that little chap would have died last night if it wasn't for you."

Andra blushed, snorting to hide his embarrassment.

"Nah, don't be daft," he said his tone dismissive but tinged with pride. "It was a joint effort!"

They watched as the lamb finished suckling and staggered to his feet, following his mother as she walked off, its tail wiggling as he skipped around her. After a moment, the lamb scampered back to the ponies, licking each of them on the nose with its little warm tongue.

Andra laughed, though his good humour disappeared with a loud rumble from his tummy.

"Gosh, I'm hungry," he said, stating the obvious.

"Come one," said Blue, taking the lead, "follow me."

Andrew threw up his head and tutted. *Gosh, she's bossy!* He thought to himself, but with a flick of his brown and white tail, he followed without argument as she headed back to the beach.

Recognising their destination, he wasn't silent for long.

"Stop moaning," hissed Blue, but her tone was kind. "I know you didn't like the taste of seaweed, but you won't starve if you eat it. And besides, last night's storm will have brought up a fresh supply."

Andra opened his mouth to protest, but she continued, not letting him get a word in.

"And before you start, I know it isn't the food you are used to, your *Royal Highness*, but that's all there is."

The unicorn pretended to mull over what she said before trotting after her. He didn't want her thinking he'd follow her every move, or she'd want to take charge next.

Blue stared ahead of her, she'd giggle if she looked at his cross face, and that would only upset him even more.

Blue was right, as they neared the beach, they could see clumps of seaweed littered the wet sand like strands of green and brown ribbon.

Blue whickered, nodding down the beach. Andra looked in the direction she indicated.

Jet and the small herd of ponies were grazing further along the bay.

"Do you want to join them?" He asked, "after all, they are your friends."

Blue shook her head, her matted forelock flopping over her eyes.

"Na," she said, "I'd rather stay here with you, if it's ok?"

"Fine by me," he grunted, his chest swelling with pride. He didn't have many friends in the Glade, if he were truthful,

Flaunia and Blue were his only friends. He nibbled at a strand of seaweed, trying hard not to pull a face as he gave it a quick chew before swallowing.

"Nice, eh?"

"Mmm," Andra lied, snatching another mouthful.

Looking around the bay as he chewed, he noticed two men pushing a boat towards the sea. He froze, nostrils flaring.

"W… what?"

Andra didn't make a sound as he started to back away, each step slow and deliberate.

Blue swivelled to see what had frightened him, but all she could see was Cassie's father and his neighbour, Frank McCloud, pushing their rowing boat out into deeper water.

"Andra, what's the matter?"

The young unicorn dragged his gaze from the two men and glanced at his friend before returning to stare at the fisherman. He watched their every move, ready to gallop off if they headed in his direction.

Andra's mouth dried up making it hard to utter a sound.

"F... F..." he stuttered.

"Fisherman?" She said, finishing his sentence.

Andra shook his head.

"Flaunia, the Green Fairy..."

Blue snorted, forcing herself to cough to hide her irritation.

"Green Fairy?" She repeated, snatching a look at her friend. She could see from his expression he believed what he was saying. "Go on, I'm listening," she said, keeping the sarcasm out of her voice. "Tell me about Flaunia."

Andra filled his lungs with salty air before speaking.

"My home, my real home is very different to this island."

"You don't say!" She retorted, cringing at the tone in her voice.

"It's," Andra fell silent for a moment, pawing at the sand with his hoof as wondered how he should describe his home. "My father is the head of the herd of unicorns living in the Forest and Glade. We've lived under the protection of the Green Fairy for hundreds of years."

Blue chewed on a mouthful of seaweed as she listened.

"Go on," she mumbled, "tell me about the Green Fairy."

Andra shrugged.

"What can I say? She's Flaunia, the Green Fairy."

Blue smothered a smile.

"She protects our home and the creatures living there."

"Have any of the creatures left before?"

Andra shook his head, a look of horror darkened his face. *How could she ask such a thing?* He wondered.

"No!" He retorted. "Why would anyone want to leave the Glade? It's perfect." After a moment he continued. "Flaunia hasn't always been the only fairy… there were others, once upon a time."

This pricked Blue's interest.

"Really? What happened?"

Andra's face clouded.

"Flaunia had three sisters, Star, the Blue Fairy who protected the creatures of the sky. Crystalia, the White Fairy of the ice and seas and the oldest fairy, Xenethe, the Red Fairy, protector of the fire breathing creatures, all long since gone.

Alongside the fairies, lived pixies, elves and gnomes, who, along with the fire breathing creatures, have disappeared from our world, hunted by humans like Cassie."

Blue shook her head. She didn't know about all humans, but, Cassie, nor her parents would never hurt a hair or feather on any creature.

"I know how much you like the little human," he continued, "but her kind have stolen more and more of our lands. Destroying everything in their path. Even hunting animals to extinction. That's why Flaunia works so hard to keep us safe." He smiled, but his expression was sad. "It's hard to believe, but a long time ago unicorns could be found grazing alongside ponies like you. Now there is one herd left. Humans have hunted us for our horns and magical powers for centuries. One day, if I am lucky enough to find my way home, I will lead my herd. Together, Flaunia and I will protect our home."

Blue was silent. She had listened to everything he has said, at times biting her tongue to stop from interrupting. Maybe, just maybe, he did come from the magical place he described, a forest and glade filled with mythical creatures and if that were true, perhaps he really was a unicorn?

"Well?"

The sound of Andra's voice dragged her from her thoughts. He was looking straight into her eyes, almost pleading with her to believe his story.

She cleared her throat before speaking.

"Umm, you are a unicorn, aren't you?" She asked, thankful the other ponies were too far away to hear.

Andra neighed with relief as he trotted around the little filly, his brown and white tail arched over his back. She believed him, *Yea!*

Along the beach, the two men had launched the boat and were struggling to row out to deeper water.

"What are they doing?" Andra asked, tossing his head in the direction of the little boat.

Blue shook her head.

"They can't afford the fuel to launch the bigger boats. They are trying to get enough food to feed their families, and if they are lucky enough to have some to spare, it'll be shared amongst the old folk."

Andra felt ashamed as he watched the boat for a while, he'd never shared anything with anyone, taking what he wanted without a care for anyone else.

The waves, whipped up by the wind, made progress slow and dangerous, tossing the small boat like a toy.

Chapter Eight

Andra had to admit, Blue was right, *as always*, he thought with a wry smile, seaweed was an acquired taste. Perhaps, if he were to eat it for the next hundred years, he might get to like it.

He snatched another mouthful, watching as the two fishermen struggled to cast their nets over the side of the boat.

He stared as the two men started to drag their nets back onto the boat. Even from this distance, he could see the nets were almost empty. He doubted there would be enough to share. He wished there was something he could do.

He turned to Blue and started to speak, but his words were fuzzy as he had a mouthful of seaweed. Time and again, his mother had told him never to speak with his mouth full. He swallowed the salty ribbons, coughing as the food caught in his throat.

Blue twitched her ears as she waited for the coughing to stop.

"Sorry," he mumbled.

"Go on," she urged, her voice soft.

"I've been wondering..."

"Bout what?" She interrupted.

"Why is the catch so poor? Is it the time of year?"

Blue's expression saddened.

"I'm not sure. Fishing has never been this bad. No one seems to know why. If things don't improve soon, crofters and livestock could starve."

Andra nodded, trying to make sense of what she had said. His stomach had rumbled almost since he arrived in this awful place, but he wasn't starving. That must be awful.

"Is there anything we can do to help Cassie and her family?" He asked, surprised he was thinking of helping a human child.

Blue pulled a face.

"I'd love to. But we're only Shetland ponies, or… in your case… a unicorn," she added as an afterthought. "The family have been hit by such a streak of bad luck."

"What do you mean?"

"It's been one thing after another," she said. "Their milk cow died during calving. In fact, they lost mother and calf. The family were devastated."

Andra nodded, as she continued talking. Ignoring his fear of humans, it was obvious how much Cassie loved all animals.

"No one could explain why the cow died, but the crofters ate well for a while. Cassie's father made sure the meat was shared with them all."

While they had been talking, the boat had landed nearby. Cassie's father clicked his tongue and patted Blue's hindquarters as he passed, his neighbour had their small catch slung over his shoulder, it was clear there wasn't enough to share.

Andra turned away as an image of the Glade and its sweet grass crept into his mind. He remembered the rabbits nibbling on daisies side by side with the herd of unicorns as they grazed. No one was hungry.

Turning, Andra gazed along the beach. Dark storm clouds were gathering. It looked as though it was going to rain, again! He sighed loudly, realising this island was going to be his home forever. He was going to stay a stubbly little pony with the matted brown and white coat, but at least he had his friend, Blue.

As night fell, the storm broke. Lightening raced across the sky, chased several moments later by the sound of rolling thunder.

Carrie was in the barn. She had begged for scraps of fish to feed the stray cats hanging around the croft. Her mother knew she'd keep on until she had her way, so gave her the heads and skin from the fish and made sure she took a lamp to light her way to the barn, warning her daughter to take care as the wind was strong.

Cassie balanced the lamp on an upturned bucket placed just inside the barn door, the flame flickered in the wind.

"Tibbs," she called, "Blackie..."

Behind her, the flame threw up strange shadows against the barn wall as it danced in the draught.

"Tibbs, Blackie, puss, puss, puss."

The two stray cats jumped down from the empty hayloft and started to rub around her legs.

Overhead, a loud clap of thunder startled the young girl. Alarmed by the sound, she slipped on the wet floor, hitting the upturned bucket as she fell. The impact knocked the lantern to the ground shattering glass spilling the oil.

Taking a second to check if she had hurt herself, Cassie dragged herself to her feet, and started to brush the dirt from her clothes, unaware the flames had ignited the oil and debris littering the floor.

Smelling smoke, Cassie turned to see the flames creeping towards the side of the barn. A scream caught in her throat as she backed further into the barn.

Chapter Nine

Walking towards the barn, Andra wrinkled his nose at the strange smell, he hadn't smelt smoke before.

Cassie screamed, the shrill sound causing Andra to throw his head up in alarm.

"Blue, did you hear that?"

The young filly listened.

Cassie screamed again, the sound trailing off as she started to cough.

"That's Cassie!" He said.

Looking towards the barn, he could see the flames licking at the hessian sack which flapped in the broken window. Beyond the flames, he could see Cassie, her face twisted with fear, too frightened to move.

She screamed again.

Andra whinnied. He galloped towards the barn with no thought for his own safety. Nearing the building he started to cough as the smoke caught at the back of his throat. He reared onto his hind legs and crashed down on the door with his front hooves. It was so rotten it didn't take much to send it crashing against the wall, before shuddering on its one remaining hinge.

The unicorn took a moment to peer through the thickening smoke. Cassie was crawling blindly on the floor, tears streaming down her face as she choked on the smoke.

Andra whinnied again. Behind him, Blue trotted backwards and forwards, too frightened to come any closer.

Hearing the commotion, Cassie's parents ran from the cottage, heading towards the barn.

Andra realised the wind was fanning the flames. The gusts caused sparks to catch on wisps of rotting foliage sprouting from the brickwork. Taking a deep breath, he walked into the barn.

Ignoring the thumping sound of his heart pounding in his chest, he shuffled into the burning building. Confused by the smoke,

Cassie was crawling away from the door, moving further and further into the barn.

Andra grabbed the neck of the girl's jumper between his teeth. Closing his eyes to block out the sight of the flames edging closer and closer to them, he started to back out of the barn, dragging the little human with him.

Cassie was panicking, making progress was slow. She thrashed about, trying to escape his grip, not realising the unicorn was trying to save her.

With each deliberate step, he dragged the girl towards the door and out of the burning building, trying to ignore the smell of his singed hair.

Helpless, Blue continued to trot up and down, whinnying in alarm.

Cassie's parents pushed past the grey filly, her mother screaming her daughter's name as she ran towards the barn.

Andra felt as though he has been dragging the girl for miles, every muscle of his body ached. Finally, he reached the door, just as the side of the barn collapsed.

Grabbing Cassie off the ground, her father carried her away from the burning building. She spluttered and coughed as the fresh air filled her lungs.

"I... I'm so sorry, Dad. I don't know what happened, I..."

Her father didn't let her finish, he hugged her tight, telling her not to worry, the barn could be re-built. If she was safe, nothing else mattered.

"Patch?"

A puzzled look crossed her father's face, "Whose Patch?" He asked.

Blue nudged Andra, urging him to step forward, ignoring the glare he threw in her direction.

"Patch," cried Cassie, clamouring to her feet, "Patch, you saved my life."

Her father glanced at his wife and then at the scruffy brown and white pony as Cassie flung her arms around the unicorn's neck.

Andra fought the urge to turn and gallop

off, allowing Cassie's parents to fuss over him,

not noticing the sky lighten behind them.

"Andra..."

Andra threw up his head, recognising that

voice. *Flaunia?* He thought, *is that really*

Flaunia, he must be dreaming?

"Andra..."

No, someone was calling his name. Andra

spun round. Behind him, Blue stared up at the

Green Fairy, enchanted by the way the fairy's

floral gown rustled like wind gently blowing

leaves on tree as she moved. Overhead, the

moon broke through the dark clouds and bathed

her in silver light. Flaunia was the most beautiful thing the pony had ever seen.

The young filly dragged her eyes from the fairy and looked at her friend, shaking her head in disbelief. Behind her, Cassie and her family gasped in astonishment, Blue wasn't dreaming, they could see her too.

"Flaunia, err, um…" anxious, Andra started to speak. He adored Flaunia, but she had the power to return him to his home or leave him here on the island, forever, he was almost too frightened to ask the one question he knew he had to ask. "H… have you come to take me home?"

Flaunia was silent for a moment, but she smiled as she looked at the unicorn.

"Yes, Andra. I have been watching you from afar," she waved her hand in a vague fashion indicating she had always been with him. "I sent you here to learn a lesson," she continued. "Watching your selfless actions over the past few days showed me that you will be ready to lead the herd whenever that time comes."

Andra stared at the floor, "But I'm not a unicorn anymore," he mumbled, his voice little more than a whisper.

Flaunia looked at the scruffy brown and white pony with the short stubby legs and smiled, "You are still beautiful," she said.

She waved her arms over the pony.

"Shetland pony, Shetland pony, you have proved your worth.

Shetland pony, Shetland pony, brave and true... Shetland pony be gone!"

Cassie, her parents and Blue watched in astonishment as Andra, bathed in green light started to spin, disappearing in a cloud of smoke.

Cassie gasped as the smoke floated away...

"Patch, you're a ..." She didn't finish the sentence, there was no need, in front of them stood a unicorn. He was stunning, with his white conical horn and beautiful gold and silver flecked coat.

Blue backed away, overwhelmed with shyness, her friend really was a unicorn.

"Are you ready to go home?" Flaunia asked.

Andra looked confused. He had dreamt of this moment since he arrived on the island, but now he knew he couldn't leave until he did something to help these humans. A smile replaced the look of confusion as an idea came to him.

He beckoned Flaunia closer, "Can you take the diamonds from my hooves?" He whispered.

Flaunia smiled.

"Of course," she said, touching the twinkling stones with her hand and scooping them off the floor. "What would you like me to do with them?" She asked, knowing the answer.

Andra nodded towards Cassie and her parents.

Flaunia placed the diamonds in the little girl's hands.

"Sell these to feed the crofters and animals for the rest of the winter. The fish will return with the spring tides."

Cassie gasped.

"How can we ever thank you?" Her father asked.

"Stay as you are. Kind to your neighbours and the animals on the island."

"Your generosity will save lives this winter. Thank you, thank you, Patch," said Cassie's father.

"His name is Andra," Flaunia smiled, patting the unicorn on the neck, "Andra, prince of the Unicorns."

Andra whispered something to Flaunia. She nodded, turning to face Blue.

"Andra has asked if you may join him. Would you like to leave the island?"

Blue didn't hesitate, neighing in response. Flaunia waved her arms as the pony disappeared in a cloud of green smoke, revealing the most beautiful unicorn Andra had ever seen, even with her different coloured eyes.

Andra and Blue nuzzled Cassie as they said their good-byes before Flaunia clapped her hands three times, disappearing in a puff of smoke.

Cassie looked at her parents.

"No one is going to believe this, are they?" She said.

Her mother shook her head, "But we know the truth, and that's what matters."

Chapter Ten

Cassie was pleased Andra and Blue had returned home, but couldn't help feeling sad, certain she would never see them again. But she was wrong.

Each Christmas Eve, one of the most magical nights of the year, Cassie would look to the top of the cliffs towering over the beach. There she would see Andra and Blue watching over her. They would bow their heads in greeting before turning and with a flick if their tails they would be gone.

Printed in Poland
by Amazon Fulfillment
Poland Sp. z o.o., Wrocław

50327795R00065